TOP SECRET!

Diary of a ~~Super~~hero
Mega

by

Steve Barlow and Steve Skidmore

PRIVATE

This diary belongs to ...

Handyman, The Handyshed
Dulux, Glos.
England, Europe
The World, The Solar System
The Milky Way, The Universe
Etc. etc.

Do not read this!

(If you do, you will be sorry.

Don't mess with a megahero!)

Illustrated by Fred Pipes

1st January

What a great New Year's party we had last night!

The gang all came over. Here's the photo I took.

We must have been well away!

Shame about Iceman. He got too close to Flame Woman. She melted his heart and the rest of him.

Just one problem. I forgot to get crisps for the party. I was far too busy saving the world.

PS – A bloke rang up today. He asked me to put out an oil tanker fire. I told him I didn't work on Bank Holidays. He'll just have to keep it going until Tuesday.

2nd January

People keep asking me why I wear my underpants over my boiler suit. What a stupid question! Everyone knows that all megaheroes do this.

Anyway, it's part of the disguise. I don't want anyone to know who I really am, do I? I mean, who would think that Kent Clarke was the same person as Handyman?

PS Saved world again.

3rd January

Saved the world *again* today. What a bore. That's the third time this week. People are dead careless.

This time, it was a problem in space. The computer in charge of a space ship went out of control. It had its laser death thingies pointed at Earth. We were all doomed!

The Prime Minister rang me up, crying his eyes out. He said I was the only one who could save the planet. (As usual.)

I said I wasn't that keen. Wayne the Boy Wonder was up at the college doing his City and Guilds Superhero course, so I'd have to carry my own tool kit.

Anyway, to cut a long story short, I said I'd do it. Easy job really. The loony computer fired a few laser bolts at me. It tickled me a bit so I kicked it into outer space with my Doc Martens.

My boiler suit got burnt a bit on re-entry. I must send it to the cleaners and have a day off.

4th January

Woke up feeling grotty. I decided not to save the world today, so I washed the Handyvan instead. Then I took my costume to the cleaners. They said it would be ready on Friday.

5th January

Cleaned the Handyshed. Wayne the Boy
Wonder helped. It now looks very tidy!

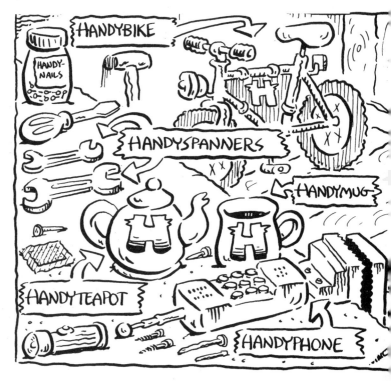

PS Didn't save the world today (for a

change!).

6th January

Rang the cleaners, but my costume isn't ready. I serviced the Handyvan instead.

The President of the United States rang to ask me if I could stop a giant meteor falling on America. I said I was sorry, but I was greasing my axle.

Then the line went dead.

I watched the news later. It said that a meteor had landed on the White House.

Ah well, there's no way I can mend the Handyvan AND save the world.

7th January

My costume still isn't ready. The cleaners think they've lost it! I'll have to find something else to wear until I get it back.

Flame Woman came over for tea. It's nice to see her, but every time she comes round she sets fire to the carpet. Today, she also burnt the armchair and my rubber plant!

8th January

Had an important call today. Someone was robbing the Bank of England. I wouldn't have bothered, but I keep my money there, so I thought I'd better sort it out.

I rang the cleaners, but my costume still wasn't ready. I had to fly round to the local Fancy Dress hire shop. I ended up hiring a pink rabbit costume.

I got there just as the robbers came out of the Bank. As soon as they saw me, they fell about laughing. It saved me the trouble of thumping them.

The problem was, when I got back to the Handyvan, it had been clamped. My Handy Bus Pass had run out, so I had to walk home. I could have flown, but who's ever heard of a flying pink rabbit? I'd have looked stupid.

9th January

Today I got a call-out to stop some mad scientist from destroying the world.

Mad Scientist

I wasn't going to wear the pink rabbit costume again, so I borrowed a pair of Flame Woman's tights. I also found a pair of curtains and a paper bag.

I stopped the mad scientist by taking his

glasses, so he couldn't see. (Strange how

all mad scientists wear glasses.)

On the way back home, I saw some bloke on top of a burning skyscraper. Decided to rescue him. I shouldn't have bothered!

Some people are never satisfied.

10th January

Bit of a job today. The new President of the United States rang up. They'd got this Giant Prehistoric Wotsit eating New York. Every time some scientist melts the ice at the North Pole, they let loose a Giant Prehistoric Wotsit. And it always eats New York. You'd think they'd learn.

It's dead boring flying over the Atlantic, especially without a plane. At least on a plane you have people bringing you drinks and things. All I had was Wayne following me on the Handybike with the tool kit.

Anyway, I gave the Giant Prehistoric Wotsit a tap on the nose with a six-pound lump hammer.

Easy, really, but I could have done without the street party afterwards. I'm just glad I didn't have to clean the mess up.

11th January

Talk about busy! I'm rushed off my feet. Some idiot brought a giant ape back from an island in the South Seas. The next thing you know, it's got some woman trapped on top of the Eiffel Tower.

It took me half the morning to sort that out. Then I had to put up with the President of France kissing me on both cheeks!

I'd hardly got my Doc Martens off when the Handyphone rang again. The QE2 had hit an iceberg and was sinking.

They wanted to know if I could come and keep it afloat while they got the Pollyfilla out.

Then I got a call to say that Concorde was about to crash. Both pilots were sick and the plane was being flown by a hairdresser from Luton called Tracey ...

Some days it just doesn't pay to get out of bed.

12th January

Hooray! At last my costume is back from the cleaners. They've still not mended the hole in the pocket, though. Anything could fall out of it. I'll have to get the Handy Sewing Kit out ...

You have found Handyman's top secret diary.

Close it at once.

If you do not, this diary will self-destruct in 10 seconds.

YOU HAVE BEEN WARNED!